DOVER
CHILDREN'S THRIFT CLASSICS

Bowser the Hound

THORNTON W. BURGESS

Original Illustrations by Harrison Cady
Adapted by Pat Stewart

P9-DMM-172

PUBLISHED IN ASSOCIATION WITH THE
THORNTON W. BURGESS MUSEUM AND THE
GREEN BRIAR NATURE CENTER, SANDWICH, MASSACHUSETTS,
BY
DOVER PUBLICATIONS, INC., MINEOLA, NEW YORK

DOVER CHILDREN'S THRIFT CLASSICS
EDITOR OF THIS VOLUME: TOM CRAWFORD

TO THE CHILD'S LOVING PLAYMATE,
LOYAL PROTECTOR
AND STAUNCH ALLY
—THE DOG,
THIS BOOK IS DEDICATED

Bibliographical Note

This Dover edition, first published in 2003 in association with the Thornton W. Burgess Museum and the Green Briar Nature Center, Sandwich, Massachusetts, who have provided a new introduction, is an unabridged republication of the text of the edition published by Little, Brown, and Company, Boston, 1920. Six of the original Harrison Cady illustrations have been adapted for this new edition by Pat Stewart.

Library of Congress Cataloging-in-Publication Data

Burgess, Thornton W. (Thornton Waldo), 1874–1965.
    Bowser the hound / Thornton W. Burgess — [1st Dover ed.]
      p. cm. — (Dover children's thrift classics)
    Summary: Chronicles the adventures of Bowser the hound with an assortment of other animals.
    ISBN 0-486-42847-8 (pbk.)
    [1. Dogs—Fiction. 2. Animals—Fiction.] I. Cady, Harrison, ill. II. Stewart, Pat, ill. III. Title. IV. Series.

PZ7.B917Bh 2003
[Fic]—dc21
                                                                    2003040965

Manufactured in the United States of America
Dover Publications, Inc., 31 East 2nd Street, Mineola, N.Y. 11501

Introduction to the Dover Edition

Bowser the Hound was written back in 1920. It was originally part of the Green Meadow Series of books. In this story, Bowser the Hound gets hopelessly lost and has many adventures away from the farm. Learn how Blacky the Crow plays an important role in helping Bowser find his way home. Mr. Burgess wrote over 170 books during his writing career. He was also a successful radio-show host, syndicated newspaper columnist, and well-known authority on nature.

Thornton W. Burgess dedicated this book *"to the child's loving playmate, loyal protector and staunch ally—the dog."* While Thornton Burgess owned a few dogs during his lifetime, he seemed to be more partial to the wild animals in the forest and woodlands. He once wrote in his autobiography, *Now I Remember,* about a neighbor's dog back when he was growing up in Sandwich. During one Christmas season Thornton Burgess took orders for Christmas cards. While canvassing the village homes, he also sold his mother's molasses candy. Like everyone else, "Old Bruce," a neighbor's pointer dog, was partial to candy. One day he slipped in to the back room where Thornton Burgess's mother had

 left a batch of molasses candy on the table to cool. Bruce took the whole batch of candy in his mouth. It had stiffened enough to be chewy and to stick to his teeth. His jaws got stuck together, and he struggled in vain to get them unstuck. That batch of candy was a total loss except for the fact that Old Bruce never again turned to stealing.

Today, you can learn more about Thornton Burgess and his early life in Sandwich by visiting the Thornton Burgess Museum or the Green Briar Nature Center or online at **www.thorntonburgess.org**. Both the Museum and Green Briar are operated by the Thornton W. Burgess Society, a non-profit educational organization founded in 1976 *"to inspire reverence for wildlife and concern for the environment."*

Contents

List of Illustrations

I
Old Man Coyote Leads Bowser Away

Though great or small the matter prove
Be faithful in whate'er you do.
'Tis thus and only thus you may
To others and yourself be true.
Bowser the Hound.

OLD Man Coyote is full of tricks. People with such clever wits as his usually are full of tricks. On the other hand Bowser the Hound isn't tricky at all. He just goes straight ahead with the thing he has to do and does it in the most earnest way. Not being tricky himself, he sometimes forgets to watch out for tricks in others.

One day he found the fresh trail of Old Man Coyote and made up his mind that he would run down Old Man Coyote if he had to run his legs off to do it. He always makes up his mind like that whenever he starts out to hunt. You know there is nothing in the world Bowser enjoys quite so much as to hunt some one who will give him a long, hard run. Any time he will go without eating for the pleasure of chasing Reddy or Granny Fox, or Old Man Coyote.

Now Old Man Coyote was annoyed. He was and he wasn't afraid of Bowser the Hound. That is to

1

say he was afraid to fight Bowser, but he wasn't afraid to be hunted by Bowser, because he was so sure that he was smart enough to get away from Bowser. If Bowser had appeared at almost any other time Old Man Coyote wouldn't have been so annoyed. But to have Bowser appear just then made him angry clear through. You see he had just started out to get his dinner.

"What business has that good-for-nothing dog over here anyway, I'd like to know," he muttered, as he ran swiftly through the Green Forest. "What right has he to meddle in other folks' business? I'll just teach that fellow a lesson; that's what I'll do! I'll teach him that he can't interfere with me and not be sorry for it."

So Old Man Coyote ran and ran and ran, and never once did he try to break his trail. In fact, he took pains to leave a trail that Bowser could follow easily. After him Bowser ran and ran and ran, and all the time his great voice rang out joyously. This was the kind of a hunt he loved. Out of the Green Forest into the Old Pasture, Old Man Coyote led Bowser the Hound. Across the Old Pasture and out on the other side they raced. Farther and farther away from home Old Man Coyote led Bowser the Hound. Instead of circling back as usual, he kept on. Bowser kept on after him. By and by he was in strange country, country he had never visited before. He didn't notice this. He didn't notice anything but the splendid trail Old Man Coyote was

This was the kind of a hunt he loved. *See page 2.*

making. He didn't even realize that he was getting
tired. Always in his nose was the tantalizing scent
of Old Man Coyote. Bowser was sure that this time
he would catch this fellow who had fooled him so
often before.

II
Old Man Coyote Plays a Trick

Of people who play tricks beware,
Lest they may get you in a snare.
You cannot trust them, so watch out
Whenever one may be about.
                    Bowser the Hound.

THERE is such a thing as being too much interested in the thing you are doing. That is the
way accidents very often happen. A person will get
so interested in something that he will be blind
and deaf to everything else, and so will walk
straight into danger or trouble of some kind.

Now just take the case of Bowser the Hound.
Bowser was so interested in the chase of Old Man
Coyote that he paid no attention whatever to anything but the warm scent of Old Man Coyote which
the latter was taking pains to leave. Bowser ran
with his nose in Old Man Coyote's tracks and never
looked either to left or right. He would lift his head
only to look straight ahead in the hope of seeing
Old Man Coyote. Then down would go his nose
again to follow that scent.

So Bowser didn't notice that Old Man Coyote
was leading him far, far away from home into country with which he was quite unacquainted. Bowser

5

has a great, deep, wonderful voice which can be heard a very long distance when he bays on the tracks of some one he is hunting. It can be heard a very long distance indeed. But far as it can be heard, Bowser was far, far beyond hearing distance from Farmer Brown's house before Old Man Coyote began to even think of playing one of his clever tricks in order to make Bowser lose his scent. You see, Old Man Coyote intended to lead Bowser into strange country and there lose him, hoping that he would not be able to find the way home.

Old Man Coyote is himself a tireless runner. He is not so heavy as is Bowser, so does not tire as easily. Then, too, he had not wasted his breath as had Bowser with his steady baying. Old Man Coyote could tell by the sound of Bowser's voice when the latter was beginning to grow tired, and he could tell by the fact that he often had a moment or two to sit down and rest before Bowser got dangerously near.

So at last Old Man Coyote decided that the time had come to play a trick. By and by he came to a river. At that point there was a high, overhanging bank. On the very edge of this bank Old Man Coyote made a long leap to one side. Then he made another long leap to the big trunk of a fallen tree. He ran along this and from the end of it made still another long leap, as long a leap as he could. Then he hid in a little thicket to see what would happen.

III
What Happened to Bowser

When a Coyote seems most honest,
watch him closest.
　　　　　Bowser the Hound.

BOWSER was very, very tired. He wouldn't admit it even to himself, for when he is hunting he will keep on until he drops if his wonderful nose can still catch the scent of the one he is following. Bowser is wonderfully persistent. So, though he was very, very tired, he kept his nose to the ground and tried to run even faster, for the scent of Old Man Coyote was so strong that Bowser felt sure he would soon catch him.

Bowser didn't look to see where he was going. He didn't care. It was enough for him to know that Old Man Coyote had gone that way, and where Old Man Coyote could go Bowser felt sure he could follow. So, still baying with all his might and making the hills ring with the sound of his great voice, Bowser kept on.

Hidden in a little thicket, stretched out so that he might rest better, Old Man Coyote listened to that great voice drawing nearer and nearer. There

7

was a wicked grin on Old Man Coyote's face, and in his yellow eyes a look of great eagerness. In a few minutes Bowser came in sight, his nose in the trail Old Man Coyote had left. Into Bowser's voice crept a new note of eagerness as his nose picked up the scent stronger than ever. Straight on he raced and it seemed as if he had gained new strength. His whole thought was on just one thing—catching Old Man Coyote, and Old Man Coyote knew it.

Bowser didn't see that he was coming to a steep bank. He didn't see it at all until he reached the edge of it, and then he was going so fast that he couldn't stop. Over he went with a frightened yelp! Down, down he fell, and landed with a thump on the ice below. He landed so hard that he broke the ice, and went through into the cold, black water.

Old Man Coyote crept to the edge of the bank and peeped over. Poor Bowser was having a terrible time. You see, the cold water had taken what little breath his fall had not knocked out of him. He doesn't like to go in water anyway. You know the hair of his coat is short and doesn't protect him as it would if it were long. Old Man Coyote grinned wickedly as he watched Bowser struggling feebly to climb out on the ice. Each time he tried he slipped back, and all the time he was whimpering.

Old Man Coyote grinned more wickedly than ever. I suspect that he hoped that Bowser would not be able to get out. But after a little Bowser did manage to crawl out, and stood on the ice, shivering and shaking. Once more Old Man Coyote grinned, then, turning, he trotted back towards Farmer Brown's.

IV
Poor Bowser

Follow a crooked trail and you will find
a scamp at the end.
Bowser the Hound.

POOR Bowser! He stood shivering and shaking on the ice of the strange river to which Old Man Coyote had led him, and he knew not which way to turn. Not only was he shivering and shaking from his cold bath, but he was bruised by his fall from the top of the steep bank, and he was so tired by his long run after Old Man Coyote that he could hardly stand.

Old Man Coyote had stayed only long enough to see that Bowser had managed to get out of the water, then had turned back towards the Old Pasture, the Green Meadows and the Green Forest near Farmer Brown's. You see, Old Man Coyote knew the way back. He would take his time about getting there, for it really made no particular difference to him when he reached home. He felt sure he would be able to find something to eat on the way.

But with Bowser it was very different. Poor Bowser didn't know where he was. It would have been bad enough under any circumstances to have been lost, but to be lost and at the same time tired almost to death, bruised and lame, wet and chilled through, was almost too much to bear. He hadn't the least idea which way to turn. He couldn't climb up the bank to find his own trail and follow it back home if he wanted to. You see, that bank was very steep for some distance in each direction, and so it was impossible for Bowser to climb it.

For a few minutes he stood shivering, shaking and whimpering, not knowing which way to turn. Then he started down the river on the ice, for he knew he would freeze if he continued to stand still. He limped badly because one leg had been hurt in his fall. After a while he came to a place where he could get up on the bank. It was in the midst of deep woods and a very, very lonely place. Hard crusted snow covered the ground, but it was better than walking on the ice and for this Bowser was thankful.

Which way should he turn? Where should he go? Night was coming on; he was wet, cold and hungry, and as utterly lost as ever a dog was. Poor Bowser! For a minute or two he sat down and howled from sheer lonesomeness and discouragement. How he did wish he had left Old Man Coyote alone! How he did long for his snug, warm, little house in Farmer Brown's dooryard, and for the good meal he knew was awaiting him there. Now that the excitement of the hunt was over, he realized how very, very hungry he was, and he began to wonder where he would be able to get anything to eat. Do you wonder that he howled?

Old Man Coyote, trotting along on his way home, heard that howl and understood it. Again he grinned that wicked grin of his, and stopped to listen. "I don't think he'll hunt me again in a hurry," he muttered, then trotted on. Poor Bowser! Hunting for anything but his home was farthest from his thoughts.

V
Bowser Spends a Bad Night

There's nothing like just sticking to
The thing you undertake to do.
There'll be no cause then, though you fail,
To hang your head or drop your tail.
Bowser the Hound.

BOWSER was lost, utterly lost. He hadn't the least idea in which direction Farmer Brown's house was. In fact he hadn't the least idea which way to turn to find any house. It was the most lonely kind of a lonely place to which Old Man Coyote had led him and there played the trick on him which had caused him to tumble into the strange river.

But Bowser couldn't stand still for long. Already jolly, round, red Mr. Sun was going to bed behind the Purple Hills, and Bowser knew that cold as had been the day, the night would be still colder. He must keep moving until he found a shelter. If he didn't he would freeze. So whimpering and whining, Bowser limped along.

Bowser was not afraid to be out at night as some folks are. Goodness, no! In fact, on many a moonlight night Bowser had hunted Reddy Fox or Granny Fox all night long. Never once had he felt lonesome then. But now it was very, very different. You see, on those nights when he had hunted he always had known where he was. He had known that at any time he could go straight home if he wanted to. That made all the difference in the world.

It would have been bad enough, being lost this way, had he been feeling at his best. Being lost always makes one feel terribly lonesome. Lonesomeness is one of the worst parts of the feeling of being lost. But added to this was the fact that Bowser was really not in fit condition to be out at all. He was wet, tired, lame and hungry. Do you wonder that he whimpered and whined as he limped along over the hard snow, and hadn't the least idea whether he was headed towards home or deeper into the great woods?

For a long time he kept on until it seemed to him he couldn't drag one foot after another. Then quite suddenly something big and dark loomed up in front of him. It really wasn't as big as it seemed. It was a little house, a sugar camp, just such a one as Farmer Brown has near his home. Bowser crept to the door. It was closed. Bowser sniffed and sniffed and his heart sank, for there was no scent of human beings. Then he knew that that little house was deserted and empty. Still he whined and scratched at the door. By and by the door opened ever so little, for it had not been locked.

Bowser crept in. In one corner he found some

hay, and in this he curled up. It was cold, very cold, but not nearly as cold as outside that little house. So Bowser curled up in the hay and shivered and shook and slept a little and wished with all his might that he never had found the tracks of Old Man Coyote.

VI
The Surprise of Blacky the Crow

The harder it is to follow a trail
The greater the reason you should not fail.
Bowser the Hound.

A T all seasons of the year Blacky the Crow is
something of a traveler. But in winter he is
much more of a traveler than in summer. You see,
in winter it is not nearly so easy to pick up a living.
Food is quite as scarce for Blacky the Crow in winter as for any of the other little people who neither
sleep the winter away nor go south. All of the
feathered folks have to work and work hard to find
food enough to keep them warm. You know it is
food that makes heat in the body.

So in the winter Blacky is in the habit of flying
long distances in search of food. He often goes
some miles from the thick hemlock-tree in the
Green Forest where he spends his nights. You may
see him starting out early in the morning and
returning late in the afternoon.

Now Blacky knew all about that river into which
Bowser the Hound had fallen. There was a certain
place on that river where Jack Frost never did succeed in making ice. Sometimes things good to eat
would be washed up along the edge of this open

16

place. Blacky visited it regularly. He was on the way there now, flying low over the tree-tops.

Presently he came to a little opening among the trees. In the middle of it was a little house, a rough little house. Blacky knew all about it. It was a sugar camp. He knew that only in the spring of the year was he likely to find anybody about there. All the rest of the year it was shut up. Every time he passed that way Blacky flew over it. Blacky's eyes are very sharp indeed, as everybody knows. Now, as he drew near, he noticed right away that the door was partly open. It hadn't been that way the last time he passed.

"Ho!" exclaimed Blacky. "I wonder if the wind blew that open, or if there is some one inside. I think I'll watch a while."

So Blacky flew to the top of a tall tree from which he could look all over the little clearing and could watch the door of the little house.

For a long time he sat there as silent as the trees themselves. Nothing happened. He began to grow tired. Rather, he began to grow so hungry that he became impatient. "If there is anybody in there he must be asleep," muttered Blacky to himself. "I'll see if I can wake him up. Caw, caw, ca-a-w, caw, caw!"

Blacky waited a few minutes, then repeated his cry. He did this three times and had just made up his mind that there was nobody inside that little house when a head appeared in the doorway.

Blacky was so surprised that he nearly fell from his perch.

"As I live," he muttered, "that is Bowser the Hound! It certainly is. Now what is he doing way over here? I've never known him to go so far from home before."

"As I live," he muttered, "that is Bowser the Hound!"
See page 18.

VII
Blacky the Crow Takes Pity on Bowser

Beneath a coat of ebon hue
May beat a heart that's kind and true.
The worst of scamps in time of need
Will often do a kindly deed.

Bowser the Hound.

"CAW, ca-a-w!" exclaimed Blacky the Crow. Bowser looked up to the top of the tall tree where Blacky sat, and in his great, soft eyes was such a look of friendliness that it gave Blacky a funny feeling. You know Blacky is not used to friendly looks. He is used to quite the other kind. Bowser came out of the old sugar house where he had spent the night and whined softly as he looked up at Blacky, and as he whined he wagged his tail ever so slightly. Blacky didn't know what to make of it. He had never been more surprised in his life. He didn't know which surprised him most, finding Bowser 'way over here where he had no business to be, or Bowser's friendliness.

As for Bowser, he had spent such a forlorn, miserable night, and he was so terribly lonesome, that the very sound of Blacky's voice had given him a queer thrill. Never had he thought of Blacky the Crow as a friend. In fact, he never thought much

20

about Blacky at all. Sometimes he had chased Blacky out of Farmer Brown's cornfield early in the spring but that is all he ever had had to do with him. Now, however, lonesome and lost as he was, the sound of a familiar voice made him tingle all over with a friendly feeling. So he whined softly and wagged his tail feebly as he looked up at Blacky sitting in the top of a tall tree. Presently Bowser limped out to the middle of the little clearing and turned first this way and then that way. Then he sat down and howled dismally. In an instant Blacky the Crow understood; Bowser was lost.

"So that's the trouble," muttered Blacky to himself. "That silly dog has got himself lost. I never will be able to understand how anybody can get lost. I never in my life was lost, and never expect to be. But it is easy enough to see that Bowser is lost and badly lost. My goodness, how lame he is! I wonder what's happened to him. Serves him right for hunting other people, but I'm sorry for him just the same. What a helpless creature a lost dog is, anyway. I suppose if he doesn't find a house pretty soon he will starve to death. Old Man Coyote wouldn't. Reddy Fox wouldn't. They would catch something to eat, no matter where they were. I suppose they wouldn't thank me for doing it, but just the same I think I'll take pity on Bowser and help him out of his trouble.

VIII
How Blacky the Crow Helped Bowser

The blackest coat may cover the kindest heart.
Bowser the Hound.

WHEN Blacky the Crow said to himself that he guessed he would take pity on Bowser and help him out of his trouble, he knew that he could do it without very much trouble to himself. Perhaps if there had been very much trouble in it, Blacky would not have been quite so ready and willing. Then again, perhaps it isn't fair to Blacky to think that he might not have been willing. Even the most selfish people are sometimes kindly and unselfish.

Blacky knew just where the nearest house was. You can always trust Blacky to know not only where every house is within sight of the places he frequents, but all about the people who live in each house. Blacky makes it his business to know these things. He could, if he would, tell you which houses have terrible guns in them and which have not. It is by knowing such things that Blacky manages to avoid danger.

"If that dog knows enough to follow me, I'll take him where he can at least get something to eat,"

22

muttered Blacky. "It won't be far out of my way, anyway, because if he has any sense at all, I won't have to go all the way over there."

So Blacky spread his black wings and disappeared over the tree-tops in the direction of the nearest farmhouse.

Bowser watched him disappear and whined sadly, for somehow it made him feel more lonesome than before. But for one thing he would have gone back to his bed of hay in the corner of that sugar camp. That one thing was hunger. It seemed to Bowser that his stomach was so empty that the very sides of it had fallen in. He just *must* get something to eat.

So, after waiting a moment or two, Bowser turned and limped away through the trees, and he limped in the direction which Blacky the Crow had taken. You see, he could still hear Blacky's voice calling "Caw, caw, caw," and somehow it made him feel better, less lonesome, you know, to be within hearing of a voice he knew.

Bowser had to go on three legs, for one leg had been so hurt in the fall over the bank that he could not put his foot to the ground. Then, too, he was very, very stiff from the cold and the wetting he had received the night before. So poor Bowser made slow work of it, and Blacky the Crow almost lost patience waiting for him to appear.

As soon as Bowser came in sight, Blacky gave what was intended for a cheery caw and then headed straight for the place he had started for that morning, giving no more thought to Bowser the Hound. You see, he knew that Bowser would shortly come to a road. "If he doesn't know enough to follow that road, he deserves to starve," thought Blacky.

Bowser did know enough to follow that road. The instant he saw that road, he knew that if he kept on following it, it would lead him somewhere. So with new hope in his heart, Bowser limped along.

IX
Old Man Coyote Gives Out Dark Hints

A little hint dropped there or here,
Is like a seed in spring of year;
It sprouts and grows, and none may say
How big 'twill be some future day.
Bowser the Hound.

AFTER leading Bowser the Hound far, far away and getting him lost in strange country, Old Man Coyote trotted back to the Old Pasture, the Green Forest, and the Green Meadows near Farmer Brown's. He didn't have any trouble at all in finding his way back. You see, all the time he was leading Bowser away, he himself was using his eyes and taking note of where he was going. You can't lose Old Man Coyote. No, Sir, you can't lose Old Man Coyote, and it is of no use to try.

So, stopping two or three times to hunt a little by the way, Old Man Coyote trotted back. He managed to pick up a good meal on the way, and when at last he reached his home in the Old Pasture he was feeling very well satisfied with the Great World in general and himself in particular.

He grinned as only Old Man Coyote can grin. "I don't think any of us will be bothered by that meddlesome Bowser very soon again," said he, as he crept into his house for a nap. "If he had drowned in that river, I shouldn't have cried over it. But even as it is, I don't think he will get back here in a hurry. I must pass the word along."

So a day or so later, when Sammy Jay happened along, Old Man Coyote asked him, in quite a matter-of-fact way, if he had seen anything of Bowser the Hound for a day or two.

"Why do you ask?" said Sammy sharply.

Old Man Coyote grinned slyly. "For no reason at all, Sammy. For no reason at all," he replied. "It just popped into my head that I hadn't heard Bowser's voice for two or three days. It set me to wondering if he is sick, or if anything has happened to him."

That was enough to start Sammy Jay straight for Farmer Brown's dooryard. Of course Bowser wasn't to be seen. Sammy hung around and watched. Twice he saw Farmer Brown's boy come to the door with a worried look on his face and heard him whistle and call for Bowser. Then there wasn't the slightest doubt in Sammy's mind that something had happened to Bowser.

"Old Man Coyote knows something about it, too," muttered Sammy, as he turned his head on one side and scratched his pointed cap thoughtfully. "He can't fool me. That old rascal knows where Bowser is, or what has happened to him, and I wouldn't be a bit surprised if he had something to do with it. I almost know he did from the way he grinned."

The day was not half over before all through the Green Forest and over the Green Meadows had spread the report that Bowser the Hound was no more.

X
How Reddy Fox Investigated

In-vest-i-gate if you would know
That something is or isn't so.
Bowser the Hound.

TO in-vest-i-gate something means to try to find
out about it. Reddy Fox had heard from so
many different ones about the disappearance of
Bowser that he finally made up his mind that he
would in-vest-i-gate and find out for himself if it
were true that Bowser was no longer at home in
Farmer Brown's dooryard. If it were true—well,
Reddy had certain plans of his own in regard to
Farmer Brown's henhouse.

Reddy had begun by doubting that story
because it seemed to have come first from Old
Man Coyote. Reddy would doubt anything with
which Old Man Coyote was concerned. But Reddy
had finally come to believe that something certainly had happened because half a dozen times
during the day he had heard Farmer Brown's boy
whistle and whistle and call and call.

Just as soon as the Black Shadows came creeping out from the Purple Hills, Reddy started up
towards Farmer Brown's. He didn't go directly

there, because he never goes directly anywhere if there is the least chance in the world that any one may be watching him. But as he slipped along in the blackest of the Black Shadows, he was all the time working nearer and nearer to Farmer Brown's dooryard. Although he was inclined to think it was true that Bowser was not there, he was far too wise to take any unnecessary risk. He approached Farmer Brown's dooryard just as carefully as if he knew Bowser to be in his little house as usual. He kept in the Black Shadows. He crouched so low that he seemed hardly more than a Black Shadow himself. Every two or three steps he stopped to look, listen, and test the air with his keen nose.

As he drew near Bowser's own little house, Reddy circled out around it until he could see the doorway. Then he sat down where he could peek around from behind a tree and watch. He had been there only a few moments when the back door of Farmer Brown's house opened and Farmer Brown's boy stepped out. Reddy didn't run. He knew that Farmer Brown's boy would never dream that he would dare come so near. Besides, it was very clear that Farmer Brown's boy was thinking of no one but Bowser. He whistled and called just as he had done several times during the day. But no Bowser came, so after a while Farmer Brown's boy went back into the house. There was a worried look on his face.

As soon as he heard the door close, Reddy

trotted right out in the open and sat down only a few feet from the black doorway of Bowser's little house. Reddy barked softly. Then he barked a little louder. He knew that if Bowser were at home, that bark would bring him out if nothing else did. Bowser didn't appear. Reddy grinned. He was sure now that Bowser was nowhere about. Chuckling to himself, he turned and trotted towards Farmer Brown's henhouse.

XI
A Little Unpleasantness

Watch a Coyote most closely when it appears
that he least needs watching.
Bowser the Hound.

NEVER in his life had Reddy Fox visited Farmer
Brown's henhouse with quite such a comfortable feeling as he now had. He knew for a certainty
that Bowser the Hound was not at home. He knew
because he had finally crept up and peeped in the
door of Bowser's little house. What had become of
Bowser he didn't know, and he didn't care. It was
enough to know that he wasn't about.

"I hope Farmer Brown's boy has forgotten to
close that little doorway where the hens run in and
out," muttered Reddy, as he trotted across Farmer
Brown's dooryard. Once he stopped, and looking
up at the lighted windows of the house, grinned.
You see, with Bowser gone, Reddy wasn't the least
bit afraid.

"If I can get into that henhouse," thought Reddy,
"I certainly will have one good feast to-night. That
is, I will if those stupid hens are not roosting so
high that I can't get them. I'll eat one right there."
Reddy's mouth watered at the very thought. "Then

I'll take one home to Mrs. Reddy. If there is time we both will come back for a couple more."

So Reddy made pleasant plans as he approached Farmer Brown's henhouse. When he reached it he paused to listen to certain sounds within, certain fretful little cluckings. Reddy sat down for a minute with his tongue hanging out and the water actually dripping from it. He could shut his eyes and see those roosts with the hens crowded together so that every once in a while one would be wakened and fretfully protest against being crowded so.

But Reddy sat there only for a minute. He was too eager to find out if it would prove to be possible to get inside that henhouse. Running swiftly but cautiously past the henhouse and along one side of the henyard, he peeped around the corner to see if by any chance the yard gate had been left open. His heart gave a leap of joy as he saw that the gate was not quite closed. All he would have to do would be to push it and enter.

Reddy turned the corner quickly. Just as he put up one paw to push the gate open, a low but decidedly ugly growl made him jump back with every hair of his coat standing on end. His first thought was of Bowser. It must be that Bowser had returned! Believing in safety first, Reddy did not stop to see who had growled, but ran swiftly a short distance. Then he looked behind him. Over at the gate of Farmer Brown's henyard he could see a dark form. At once Reddy knew that it wasn't

Over at the gate of Farmer Brown's henyard
he could see a dark form. *See page 32.*

Bowser the Hound, for it had a bushy tail, while Bowser's was smooth. Reddy knew who it was. It was Old Man Coyote.

XII
The Cleverness of Old Man Coyote

Who thinks the quickest and the best
Is bound to win in every test.
Bowser the Hound.

THE meeting of Reddy Fox and Old Man Coyote just outside the gate to Farmer Brown's henyard had been wholly unexpected to both. Reddy had been so eager to get inside that gate that when he turned the corner at the henyard he hadn't looked beyond the gate. If he had looked beyond, he would have seen Old Man Coyote just coming around the other corner. As for Old Man Coyote, he had been so surprised at the sight of Reddy Fox that he had growled before he had had time to think. He was sorry the very instant he did it.

"That certainly was a stupid thing to do," muttered Old Man Coyote to himself, as he watched Reddy Fox run away in a panic. "I should have kept out of sight and let him open that gate and go inside first. There may be traps in there, for all I know. When there's likely to be danger, always let some one else find it out for you if you can." Old Man Coyote grinned as he said this.

Reddy Fox sat down at a safe distance to watch

35

what Old Man Coyote would do. Inside, Reddy was fairly boiling with disappointment and anger. He felt that he hated Old Man Coyote more than he hated anybody else he knew of. He hated him, yet there wasn't a thing he could do about it. He didn't dare fight Old Man Coyote. All he could do was to sit there at a safe distance and watch.

The gate of the henyard was open two or three inches. For a long time Old Man Coyote stood looking through that little opening. Once or twice he thrust his nose out and sniffed cautiously around the gate, but he took the greatest care not to touch it. Finally he turned and trotted away towards the Green Forest. Reddy sat right where he was, so surprised that he couldn't even think. He waited a long time to see if Old Man Coyote would return, but Old Man Coyote didn't return, and at last Reddy cautiously crept towards that unlocked gate. "I do believe that fellow didn't know enough to push that gate open," muttered Reddy to himself. "I always supposed Old Man Coyote was smart, but if this is an example of his smartness I'll match my wits against his any day."

All this time Old Man Coyote was not so far away as Reddy thought. He had gone only far enough to make sure that Reddy couldn't see him. Then, creeping along in the blackest of the Black Shadows, he had returned to a place where he could watch Reddy.

"It's queer that gate should have been left

unlocked," thought Old Man Coyote. "It may have been an accident, and again it may have been done purposely. There may not be any danger inside; then again there may. I'm not going to push that gate open or step inside when there is some one to do it for me. I'll just leave it for Reddy Fox to do."

XIII
The Mischievous Little Night Breeze

A little act of mischief can
Upset the deepest, best laid plan.
Bowser the Hound.

REDDY Fox was very pleased with himself as he thought how much smarter he was than Old Man Coyote. He didn't waste any time in pushing open the henyard gate. It didn't enter his head that there might be a trap inside. He was so eager to find out if the little door where in daytime the hens ran in and out of the henhouse was open, that he jumped inside the henyard just as soon as the gate was pushed open wide enough for him to enter.

Old Man Coyote, watching from his hiding place, saw Reddy push the gate open and enter the henyard. "So far, so good," muttered Old Man Coyote to himself. "There isn't any trap just inside that gate, so it will be safe enough for me to follow Reddy in there. I think I'll wait a bit, however, and see what luck he has in getting into the henhouse. If he catches a chicken he won't stop to eat it there. He won't dare to. All I need do is to wait right here around the corner, and if he brings a chicken out, I'll simply tell him to drop it. Then I will have the chicken and will have run no risk." You see Old Man Coyote is a very, very clever old sinner.

So Old Man Coyote peeked through the wires and watched Reddy Fox, who thought himself so much smarter, steal swiftly across to the henhouse and try that little door. It was closed, but it wasn't fastened, as Reddy could tell by poking at it.

"It is just a matter of time and patience," muttered Reddy to himself. "If I keep at it long enough, I can work it open." You see Reddy had done that very thing once before a great while ago.

So he set himself to work with such patience as he could, and all the time Old Man Coyote watched and wondered what Reddy was doing. He guessed that Reddy was having some trouble, but also he knew from Reddy's actions that Reddy hoped to get inside that henhouse.

Now Reddy had left the henyard gate ajar. If he had pushed it wide open things might have been different. But he didn't push it wide open. He left it only halfway open. By and by there happened along a mischievous little Night Breeze. There is nothing that a mischievous little Night Breeze enjoys more than making things move. This mischievous little Night Breeze found that that gate would swing, so it blew against that gate and blew and blew until suddenly, with a sharp little click, the gate closed and the spring latch snapped into place. Reddy Fox was a prisoner!

XIV

The Difference between Being
Inside and Outside

You'll find 'twill often come about
That he who's in fain would be out.
Bowser the Hound.

IT certainly is queer what a difference there is
between being inside and outside. Sometimes
happiness is inside and sometimes it is outside.
Sometimes the one who is inside wishes with all
his might that he were outside, and sometimes the
one who is outside would give anything in the
world to be inside.

Just take the case of Reddy Fox. He had stolen
inside of Farmer Brown's henyard, leaving the gate
halfway open. He had set himself to work to open
the little sliding door through which in the daytime
the hens passed in and out of the henhouse. As he
worked, he had been filled with great contentment
and joy. He knew that Bowser the Hound had disappeared. He felt sure that there was nothing to
fear, and he fully expected to dine that night on
chicken. Then along came a mischievous little
Night Breeze and swung that gate shut.

At the click of the latch Reddy turned his head,

40

and in a flash he saw what had happened. All in an instant everything had changed for Reddy Fox. Fear and despair took the place of contentment and happy anticipations. He was a prisoner inside that henyard.

Frantically Reddy rushed over to the gate. There wasn't even a crack through which he could thrust his sharp little nose. Then, beside himself with fear, he raced around that henyard, seeking a hole through which he might escape. There wasn't any hole. That fence had been built to keep out such people as Reddy Fox, and of course a fence that would keep Reddy out would also keep him in, if he happened to be caught inside as he now was. He couldn't dig down under it, because, you know, the ground was frozen hard and covered with snow and an icy crust. He was caught, and that was all there was to it.

Suddenly Reddy became aware of some one just outside the wire fence, looking in and grinning wickedly. It was Old Man Coyote. Between them was nothing but that wire, but, oh, what a difference! Reddy was inside and a prisoner. Old Man Coyote was outside and free.

"Good evening, Reddy," said Old Man Coyote. "I hope you'll enjoy your chicken dinner. When you are eating it, just think over this bit of advice: Never take a risk when you can get some one else to take it for you. I would like a chicken dinner myself, but as it is, I think I will enjoy a Mouse or two better. Pay my respects to Farmer Brown's boy when he comes in the morning."

With this, Old Man Coyote once more grinned that wicked grin of his and trotted away towards the Green Forest. Reddy watched him disappear and would have given anything in the world to have been outside the fence in his place instead of inside, where he then was.

XV
Reddy's Forlorn Chance

This saying is both true and terse:
There's nothing bad but might be worse.
                                    Bowser the Hound.

IF any one had said this to Reddy Fox during the first half hour after he discovered that he was a prisoner in Farmer Brown's henyard, he wouldn't have believed it. He wouldn't have believed a word of it. He would have said that he couldn't possibly have been worse off than he was.

He was a prisoner, and he couldn't possibly get out. He knew that in the morning Farmer Brown's boy would certainly discover him. It couldn't be otherwise. That is, it couldn't be otherwise as long as he remained in that henyard. There wasn't a thing, not one solitary thing, under or behind which he could hide. So, to Reddy's way of thinking, things couldn't possibly have been worse.

But after a while, having nothing else to do, Reddy began to think. Now it is surprising how thinking will change matters. One of the first thoughts that came to Reddy was that he might have been caught in a trap—one of those cruel traps that close like a pair of jaws and sometimes

43

break the bones of the foot or leg, and from which there is no escape. Right away Reddy realized that to have been so caught would have been much worse than being a prisoner in Farmer Brown's henyard. This made him feel just a wee, wee bit better, and he began to do some more thinking.

For a long time his thinking didn't help him in the least. At last, however, he remembered the chicken dinner he had felt so sure he was going to enjoy. The thought of the chicken dinner reminded him that inside the henhouse it was dark. He had been inside that henhouse before, and he knew that there were boxes in there. If he were inside the henhouse, it might be, it just might possibly be, that he could hide when Farmer Brown's boy came in the morning.

So once more Reddy went to work at that little sliding door where the hens ran in and out during the day. He already had found out that it wasn't fastened, and he felt sure that with patience he could open it. So he worked away and worked away, until at last there was a little crack. He got his claws in the little crack and pulled and pulled. The little crack became a little wider. By and by it was wide enough for him to get his whole paw in. Then it became wide enough for him to get his head half in. After this, all he had to do was to force himself through, for as he pushed and shoved, the little door opened. He was inside at last! There was a chance, just a forlorn chance, that he might be able to escape the notice of Farmer Brown's boy in the morning.

XVI
Why Reddy Went without a Chicken Dinner

A dinner is far better lost
Than eaten at too great a cost.
Bowser the Hound.

CAN you imagine Reddy Fox with a chicken dinner right before him and not touching it? Well, that is just what happened in Farmer Brown's henhouse. It wasn't because Reddy had no appetite. He was hungry, very hungry. He always is in winter. Then it doesn't often happen that he gets enough to eat at one meal to really fill his stomach. Yet here he was with a chicken dinner right before him, and he didn't touch it.

You see it was this way: Reddy's wits were working very fast there in Farmer Brown's henhouse. He knew that he had only a forlorn chance of escaping when Farmer Brown's boy should come to open the henhouse in the morning. He knew that he must make the most of that forlorn chance. He knew that freedom is a thousand times better than a full stomach.

On one of the lower roosts sat a fat hen. She was within easy jumping distance. Reddy knew that with one quick spring she would be his. If the hen-

46

yard gate had been open, he would have wasted no time in making that one quick spring. But the hen-yard gate, as you know, was closed fast.

"I'm awfully hungry," muttered Reddy to himself, "but if I should catch and eat that fat hen, Farmer Brown's boy would be sure to notice the feathers on the floor the very minute he opened the door. It won't do, Reddy; it won't do. You can't afford to have the least little thing seem wrong in this hen-house. What you have got to do is to swallow your appetite and keep quiet in the darkest corner you can find."

So Reddy Fox spent the rest of the night curled up in the darkest corner, partly behind a box. All the time his nose was filled with the smell of fat hens. Every little while a hen who was being crowded too much on the roost would stir uneas-ily and protest in a sleepy voice. Just think of what Reddy suffered. Just think how you would feel to be very, very hungry and have right within reach the one thing you like best in all the world to eat and then not dare touch it. Some foolish folks in Reddy's place would have eaten that dinner and trusted to luck to get out of trouble later. But Reddy was far too wise to do anything of that kind.

Doing as Reddy did that night is called exercising self-restraint. Everybody should be able to do it. But it sometimes seems as if very many people cannot do it. Anyway, they don't do it, and because they don't do it they are forever getting into trouble.

Reddy knew when morning came, although the henhouse was still dark. Somehow or other hens always know just when jolly, round, red Mr. Sun kicks his blankets off and begins his daily climb up in the blue, blue sky. The big rooster on the topmost perch stretched his long neck, flapped his wings, and crowed at the top of his voice. Reddy shivered. "It won't be long now before Farmer Brown's boy comes," thought he.

XVII
Farmer Brown's Boy Drops a Pan of Corn

Who when surprised keeps calm and cool
Is one most difficult to fool.
Bowser the Hound.

IN his lifetime Reddy Fox has spent many anxious
moments, but none more anxious than those in
which he waited for Farmer Brown's boy to open
the henhouse and feed the biddies on this particular morning.

From the moment when the big rooster on the
topmost perch stretched forth his neck, flapped
his wings, and crowed as only he can crow, Reddy
was on pins and needles, as the saying is. Hiding
behind a box in the darkest corner of the henhouse, he hardly dared to breathe. You see, he
didn't want those hens to discover him. He knew
that if they did they would make such a racket that
they would bring Farmer Brown's boy hurrying out
to find out what the trouble was.

Reddy had had experience with hens before. He
knew that if Farmer Brown's boy heard them making a great racket, he would know that something
was wrong, and he would come all prepared. This
was the one thing that Reddy did not want. His one

49

chance to escape would be to take Farmer Brown's boy entirely by surprise.

Never had time dragged more slowly. The hens were awake, and several of them flew down to the floor of the henhouse. They passed so close to where Reddy was hiding that merely by reaching out a black paw he could have touched them. Because he took particular pains not to move, not even to twitch a black ear, they did not see him. Anyway, if they did see him, they took no notice of him. How the moments did drag! All the time he lay there listening, wishing that Farmer Brown's boy would come, yet dreading to have him come. It seemed ages before he heard sounds which told him that people were awake in Farmer Brown's house.

Finally he heard a distant door slam. Then he heard a whistle, a merry whistle. It drew nearer and nearer; Farmer Brown's boy was coming to feed the hens. Reddy tried to hold his breath. He heard the click of the henyard gate as Farmer Brown's boy opened it, then he heard the crunch, crunch, crunch of Farmer Brown's boy's feet on the snow.

Suddenly the henhouse door was thrown open and Farmer Brown's boy stepped inside. In his hand he held a pan filled with the breakfast he had brought for the hens. Suddenly a box in the darkest corner of the henhouse moved. Farmer Brown's boy turned to look, and as he did so a slim form dashed fairly between his legs. It startled him so that he dropped the pan and spilled the corn all over the henhouse floor. "Great Scott!" he exclaimed. "What under the sun was that?" and rushed to the door to see. He was just in time to get a glimpse of a red coat and a bushy tail disappearing around a corner of the barn.

XVIII
Mutual Relief

The wise Fox knows that with every chicken he steals he puts an increased price on his own skin.

Bowser the Hound.

WHEN Reddy Fox dashed between the legs of Farmer Brown's boy and out of the open door of the henhouse, it was with his heart in his mouth. At least, it seemed that way. Would he find the henyard gate open? Supposing Farmer Brown's boy had closed it after he entered! Reddy would then be a prisoner just as he had been all night, and all hope would end.

Just imagine with what terrible anxiety and eagerness Reddy looked towards that gate as he dashed out of the open door. Just imagine the relief that was his when he saw that the gate was open. In that very instant the snowy outside world became more beautiful and wonderful than ever it had been in all his life before. He was free! free! free!

If ever there was a surprised boy, that boy was Farmer Brown's as he watched Reddy twist around a corner of the barn and disappear.

"Reddy Fox!" he exclaimed. "Now how under the

sun did that rascal get in here?" Then, as he realized that Reddy had actually been inside the henhouse, anxiety for the biddies swept over him.
Hastily he turned, fully expecting to see either the
bodies of two or three hens on the floor, or scattered feathers to show that Reddy had enjoyed a
midnight feast. There were no feathers, and so far
as he could see, all the hens were standing or walking about.

At once Farmer Brown's boy began to count
them. Of course, he knew exactly how many there
should be. When he got through counting, not one
was missing. Farmer Brown's boy was puzzled. He
counted them again. Then he counted them a third
time. He began to think there must be something
wrong with his counting. After the fourth count,
however, he was forced to believe that not a single
one was missing.

If Reddy Fox had been relieved when he discovered that henyard gate open, Farmer Brown's boy
was equally relieved when he found that not a single biddie had been taken. When two people are
relieved at the same time, it is called mutual relief.
But there was this difference between Reddy Fox
and Farmer Brown's boy: Reddy knew all about
what had happened, and Farmer Brown's boy
couldn't even guess. He went all around that henhouse, trying to find a way by which Reddy Fox
had managed to get in. Of course, he discovered
that the little sliding door where the biddies go in

and out of the henhouse was open. He guessed that this was the way by which Reddy had entered.

But this didn't explain matters at all. He knew that the gate had been latched when he entered the henyard that morning. How had Reddy managed to get into that henyard with that gate closed? To this day, Farmer Brown's boy is still wondering.

XIX
Where Was Bowser the Hound?

A good Hound never barks on a cold trail.
Bowser the Hound.

WHERE was Bowser the Hound? That was the question which was puzzling all the little people who knew him. Also it was puzzling Farmer Brown's boy and Farmer Brown and Mrs. Brown. I have said that it was puzzling all the little people who knew him. This is not quite true, because there were two who could at least guess what had become of Bowser. One was Old Man Coyote, who had, as you remember, led Bowser far away and got him lost. The other was Blacky the Crow, who had discovered Bowser in his trouble and had helped him.

Old Man Coyote didn't know exactly where Bowser was, and he wasn't interested enough to think much about it. He hoped that Bowser had been so badly lost that he never would return. Blacky the Crow knew exactly where Bowser was, but he kept it to himself. It pleases Blacky to have a secret which other people would give much to know. Blacky is one of those people who can keep a secret. He isn't at all like Peter Rabbit.

Reddy Fox was one who was very much interested in the fate of Bowser the Hound. As day after day went by and Bowser did not appear, Reddy had a growing hope that he never would appear.

"I can't imagine what Old Man Coyote could have done to Bowser," said Reddy to himself. "He certainly couldn't have killed Bowser in a fight, for that old rascal would never in the world dare face Bowser the Hound in a fight. But he certainly has caused something to happen to Bowser. If that bothersome dog never returns, it certainly will make things a lot easier for Granny Fox and myself."

As for Farmer Brown's boy, he was as much puzzled as any of the little people and a whole lot more worried. He drove all about the neighborhood, asking at every house if anything had been seen of Bowser. Nowhere did he get any trace of him. No one had seen him. It was very mysterious. Farmer Brown's boy had begun to suspect that Bowser had met with an accident somewhere off in the woods and had been unable to get help. It made Farmer Brown's boy very sad indeed. His cheery whistle was no longer heard, for he did not feel like whistling. At last he quite gave up hope of ever again seeing Bowser.

XX
Where Bowser Was

When things are at their very worst,
As bad, you think, as they can be,
Just lay aside your feelings sad;
The road ahead may turn, you see.
Bowser the Hound.

YOU remember that Blacky the Crow led poor Bowser to an old road and there left him. Blacky reasoned that if Bowser had any sense at all, he would know that that road must lead somewhere and would follow it. If he didn't have sense enough to do this, he deserved to starve or freeze, was the way Blacky reasoned it out. Of course Blacky knew exactly where the road would lead.

Now Bowser did have sense. Of course he did. The minute he found that road, a great load was taken from his mind. He no longer felt wholly lost. He was certain that all he had to do was to keep in that road, and sooner or later he would come to a house. The thing that worried him most was whether or not he would have strength enough to keep going until he reached that house. You remember that he was weak from lack of food, lame, and half frozen.

Poor old Bowser! He certainly was the picture of misery as he limped along that road. His tail hung down as if he hadn't strength enough to hold it up. His head also hung low. He walked on three legs and limped with one of these. In his eyes was such a look of pain and suffering as would have touched the hardest heart. He whined and whimpered as he limped along.

It seemed to him that he had gone a terribly long distance, though really it was not far at all, when something tickled his nose, that wonderful nose which can smell the tracks of others long after they have passed. But this time it wasn't the smell of a track that tickled his nose; it was something in the air. Bowser lifted his head and sniffed long and hard. What he smelled was smoke. He knew what that meant. Somewhere not very far ahead of him was a house.

With new hope and courage Bowser tried to hurry on. Presently around a turn of the road he saw a farmyard. The smell of the smoke from the chimney of the farmhouse was stronger now, and with it was mingled an appetizing smell of things cooking. Into Bowser's whimper there now crept a little note of eagerness as he dragged himself across the farmyard and up to the back door. There his strength quite left him. He didn't have enough left to even bark. All he could do was

Somewhere not very far ahead of him was a house.
See page 58.

whine. After what seemed a long, long time the door opened, and a motherly woman stood looking down at him. Two minutes later Bowser lay on a mat close by the kitchen stove.

XXI
Bowser Becomes a Prisoner

There is no one in all the Great World more faithful
than a faithful dog.

Bowser the Hound.

BOWSER the Hound was a prisoner. Yes, Sir,
Bowser was a sure-enough prisoner. But there
is a great difference in prisons. Bowser was a prisoner of kindness. It seems funny that kindness
should ever make any one a prisoner, but it is so
sometimes.

You see, it was this way: When Bowser had
been taken in to that strange farmhouse, he had
been so used up that he had had only strength
enough to very feebly wag his tail. Right away the
people in that farmhouse knew what had happened to Bowser. That is, they knew part of what
had happened to him. They knew that he had
been lost and had somehow hurt one leg. They
were very, very good to him. They fed him, and
made a comfortable bed for him, and rubbed
something on the leg which he had hurt and
which had swollen. Almost right away after eating

Bowser went to sleep and slept and slept and slept. It was the very best thing he could have done.

The next day he felt a whole lot better, but he was so stiff and lame that he could hardly move. He didn't try very much. He was petted and cared for quite as tenderly as he would have been at his own home. So several days passed, and Bowser was beginning to feel more like himself. The more he felt like himself, the more he wanted to go home. It wasn't that there he would receive any greater kindness than he was now receiving, but home is home and there is no place like it. So Bowser began to be uneasy.

"This dog doesn't belong anywhere around here," said the man of the house. "I know every Hound for miles around, and I never have seen this one before. He has come a long distance. It will not do to let him go, for he will try to find his way home and the chances are that he will again get lost. We must keep him in the house or chained up. Perhaps some day we may be able to find his owner. If not, we will keep him. I am sure he will soon become contented here."

Now that man knew dogs. Had Bowser had the chance, he would have done exactly what that man had said. He would have tried to find his way home, and he hadn't the least idea in the world in which direction home lay. But he didn't get the chance to try. When he was allowed to run out of doors it was always with some one to watch him. He was petted and babied and made a great deal of, but he knew all the time that he was a prisoner. He knew that if he was to get away at all he would have to sneak away, and somehow there never seemed a chance to do this. He was grateful to these kindly people, but down in his heart was a great longing for Farmer Brown's boy and *home*. He always felt this longing just a wee bit stronger when Blacky the Crow passed over and cawed.

XXII
Farmer Brown's Boy Looks in Vain

Loyalty is priceless and
Is neither sold nor bought.
Alas, how few who seem to know
Its value as they ought.
Bowser the Hound.

AS I have told you, Farmer Brown's boy had been all about the neighborhood asking at each farmhouse if anything had been seen of Bowser. Of course nothing had been seen of him, and so at last Farmer Brown's boy felt sure that something dreadful had happened to Bowser in the woods.

For several days he tramped through the Green Forest and up through the Old Pasture, looking for signs of Bowser. His heart was heavy, for you know Bowser was quite one of the family. He visited every place he could think of where he and Bowser had hunted together. He knew that by this time Bowser couldn't possibly be alive if he had been caught by a foot in a trap or had met with an accident in the woods. He had quite given up all hope of ever seeing Bowser alive again. But he did want to know just what had happened to him, and so he kept searching and searching.

One day Farmer Brown's boy heard that a strange dog had been found over in the next township. That afternoon he drove over there, his heart filled with great hope. But he had his long ride for nothing, for when he got there he found that the strange dog was not Bowser at all.

Meanwhile Old Man Coyote and Reddy Fox and Old Granny Fox had become very bold. They even came up around the henyard in broad daylight.

"I believe you know something about what has become of Bowser," Farmer Brown's boy said, as he chased Old Man Coyote away one day. "You certainly know that he isn't home, and I more than suspect that you know *why* he isn't home. I certainly shall have to get another dog to teach you not to be so bold."

But somehow Farmer Brown's boy couldn't bring himself quite to taking such a step as getting a new dog. He felt that no other dog ever could take Bowser's place, and in spite of the fact that he thought he had given up all hope of ever seeing Bowser again, 'way down deep inside was something which, if it were not hope, was something enough like it to keep him from getting another dog in Bowser's place.

Whenever he went about away from home, he kept an eye out for dogs in the farmyards he passed. He did it without really thinking anything about it. He had given up hope of finding Bowser, yet he was always looking for him.

XXIII
Bowser's Great Voice

To long for home when far away
Will rob of joy the brightest day.
Bowser the Hound.

THERE is as much difference in the voices of dogs as in the voices of human beings. For that matter, this is true of many of the little people who wear fur. Bowser the Hound had a wonderful, deep, clear voice, a voice that could be heard a great distance. No one who knew it would ever mistake it for the voice of any other Hound.

As a rule, Bowser seldom used that great voice of his save when he was hunting some one. Then, when the scent was strong, he gave tongue so fast that you wondered how he had breath enough left to run. But now that he was a prisoner of kindness, in the home of the people who had taken him in when he had crept to their doorstep, Bowser sometimes bayed from sheer homesickness. When he was tied out in the yard, he would sometimes get to thinking of his home and long to see Farmer Brown and Mrs. Brown and especially his master, Farmer Brown's boy. Then, when he could stand it no longer, he would open his mouth and send his great voice rolling across to the woods with a tone of mournfulness which never had been there before.

But great as was Bowser's voice, and far as it would carry, there was none who knew him to hear it, save Blacky the Crow. You remember that Blacky knew just where Bowser was and often flew over that farmyard to make sure that Bowser was still there. So more than once Blacky heard Bowser's great voice with its mournful note, and understood it.

It troubled Blacky. Yes, Sir, it actually troubled Blacky. He knew just what was the matter with Bowser, but for the life of him he couldn't think of any way of helping Bowser. "That dog is homesick," croaked Blacky, as he sat in the top of a tall tree, scratching his head as if he thought he might scratch an idea out of it. "Of course he doesn't know how to get home, and if he tried he probably would get as badly lost as he was before. Anyway, they don't give him a chance to try. I can't lead Farmer Brown's boy over here because he doesn't understand my talk, and I don't understand his. There isn't a thing I can do but keep watch. I wish Bowser would stop barking. It makes me feel uncomfortable. Yes, Sir, it makes me feel uncomfortable. Old Man Coyote got Bowser into this trouble, and he ought to get him out again, but I don't suppose it is the least bit of use to ask him. It won't do any harm to try, anyway."

So Blacky started back for the Green Forest and the Old Pasture near Farmer Brown's to look for Old Man Coyote, and for a long time as he flew he could hear Bowser's voice with its note of homesickness and longing.

XXIV

Blacky Tries to Get Help

You'll find that nothing more worth while can be
Than helping others whose distress you see.
Bowser the Hound.

ON his way back to the Green Forest near
Farmer Brown's home, Blacky the Crow kept a
sharp watch for Old Man Coyote. But Old Man Coyote was nowhere to be seen, and it was too late to
go look for him, because jolly, round, red Mr. Sun
had already gone to bed behind the Purple Hills
and the Black Shadows were hurrying towards the
Green Forest.

Blacky never is out after dark. You might think
that one with so black a coat would be fond of the
Black Shadows, but it isn't so at all. The fact is,
bold and impudent as Blacky the Crow is in daylight, he is afraid of the dark. He is quite as timid as
anybody I know of in the dark. So Blacky always
contrives to go to bed early and is securely hidden
away in his secret roosting-place by the time the
Black Shadows reach the edge of the Green Forest.

Perhaps it isn't quite fair to say that Blacky is
afraid of the dark. It isn't the dark itself that Blacky
fears, but it is one who is abroad in the dark. It is
Hooty the Owl. Hooty would just as soon dine on

Blacky the Crow as he would on any one else, and Blacky knows it.

The next morning, bright and early, Blacky flew over to the Old Pasture to the home of Old Man Coyote. Just as he got there he saw Old Man Coyote coming home from an all-night hunt. "I hope you have had good hunting," said Blacky politely.

Old Man Coyote looked up at Blacky sharply. Blacky is polite only when he wants to get something. "There was plenty of hunting, but little enough reward for it," replied Old Man Coyote. "What brings you over here so early? I should suppose you would be looking for a breakfast."

Now Blacky the Crow is a very wise fellow. He knows when it is best to be sly and crafty and when it is best to be frank and outspoken. This was a time for the latter. "I know where Bowser the Hound is," said Blacky. "I saw him yesterday."

Old Man Coyote pricked up his ears and grinned. "I thought he was dead," said he. "It's a long time since we've heard from Bowser. Is he well?"

"Quite well," replied Blacky, "but unhappy. He is homesick. I suspect that the trouble with Bowser is that he hasn't the least idea in which direction home lies. You enjoy running, so why not go with me to pay Bowser a visit and then lead him back home?"

Old Man Coyote threw back his head and laughed in that crazy fashion of his till the very hills rang with the sound of his voice.

XXV
Blacky Calls on Reddy Fox

Saying what you mean, and meaning what you say
Are matters quite as different as night is from the day.
Bowser the Hound.

BLACKY the Crow wasted no time with Old Man Coyote after he heard Old Man Coyote laugh. There was a note in that crazy laugh of Old Man Coyote's that told Blacky he might just as well talk to the rocks or the trees about helping Bowser the Hound. Old Man Coyote had led Bowser into his trouble, and it was quite clear that not only did he have no regrets, but he was actually glad that Bowser was not likely to return.

"You're a hard-hearted old sinner," declared Blacky, as he prepared to fly in search of Reddy Fox.

Old Man Coyote grinned. "It is every one for himself, you know," said he. "Bowser would do his best to catch me if he had the chance. So if he is in trouble, he can stay there for all of me."

It didn't take Blacky long to find Reddy Fox. You see, it was so early in the morning that Reddy had not retired for his daily nap. Like Old Man Coyote, he was just returning from a night's hunt when Blacky arrived.

"Hello, Reddy!" exclaimed Blacky. "You certainly

71

are looking in mighty fine condition. That red coat of yours is the handsomest coat I've ever seen. If I had a coat like that I know I should be so swelled up with pride that I just wouldn't be able to see common folks. I'm glad you're not that way, Reddy. One of the things I like about you is the fact that you never allow your fine coat to make you proud. That is more than I can say for some folks I know."

Reddy Fox sat down with his big bushy tail curled around to keep his toes warm, cocked his head on one side, and looked up at Blacky the Crow as if he were trying to see right inside that black head to find out what was going on there.

"Now what has that black scamp got in his mind," thought Reddy. "He never pays compliments unless he wants something in return. That old black rascal has the smoothest tongue in the Green Forest. He hasn't come 'way over here just to tell me that I have a handsome coat. He wouldn't fly over a fence to tell anybody that unless it was for a purpose."

Aloud he said, "Good morning, Blacky. I suppose I must admit I have a fine coat. Perhaps I do look very fine, but if you could see under this red coat of mine, you would find mighty little meat on my ribs. To be quite honest, I am not feeling half as fine as I look. You lucky fellows who can fly and don't have to think about distances may be able to live well these days, but as for me, I've forgotten when last I had a good meal."

XXVI
Red Wits and Black Wits

This fact you'll find is always so:
He's quick of wit who fools a Crow.
Bowser the Hound.

THERE is no greater flatterer in the Green Forest or on the Green Meadows than Blacky the Crow when he hopes to gain something thereby. His tongue is so smooth that it is a wonder it does not drip oil. He is crafty, is Blacky. But these same things are true of Reddy Fox. No one ever yet had a chance to accuse Reddy Fox of lacking in sharp wits. Mistakes he makes, as everybody does, but Reddy's wits are always keen and active.

Now Reddy knew perfectly well that Blacky wanted something of him, and this was why he was saying such pleasant things. Blacky the Crow knew that Reddy knew this thing, and that if he would make use of Reddy as he hoped to, he must contrive to keep Reddy wholly in the dark as to what he wanted done.

So as they sat there, Reddy Fox on the snow with his tail curled around his feet to keep them warm, and Blacky the Crow in the top of a little tree above Reddy's head, they were playing a sort of game. It

73

was red wits against black wits. Reddy was trying to outguess Blacky, and Blacky was trying to outguess Reddy, and both were enjoying it. People with sharp wits always enjoy matching their wits against other sharp wits.

When Reddy Fox said that in spite of his fine appearance he had forgotten when last he had had a good meal, Blacky pretended to think he was joking. "You surprise me," said he. "Whatever is the matter with my good friend Reddy, that he goes hungry when he no longer has anything to fear from Bowser the Hound. By the way, I saw Bowser the other day."

At this, just for an instant, Reddy's eyes flew wide open. Then they half closed again until they were just two yellow slits. But quickly as he closed them, Blacky had seen that startled surprise. "Yes," said Blacky, "I saw Bowser the other day, or at least some one who looked just like him. Wouldn't you like to have him back here, Reddy?"

"Most decidedly no," replied Reddy with great promptness. "A dog is a nuisance. He isn't of any use in the wide, wide world."

"Not even to drive off Old Man Coyote?" asked Blacky slyly, for he knew that more than once Bowser the Hound had helped Reddy out of trouble with Old Man Coyote.

Reddy pretended not to hear this. "I don't believe you saw Bowser," said he. "I don't believe anybody will ever see Bowser again. I hope not, anyway." And Blacky knew by the way Reddy said this that it would be quite useless to ask Reddy to help get Bowser home.

XXVII
The Artfulness of Blacky

Who runs in circles never gets far.
Bowser the Hound.

TO be artful is to be very clever. It is to do things in a way so clever that people will not see what you are really doing. No one can be more artful than Blacky the Crow when he sets out to be.

Blacky was smart enough not to let Reddy know that he was seeking Reddy's help for Bowser. He soon found out that Reddy would not knowingly help the least little bit, so he decided at once that the only thing for him to do was to get Reddy to help unsuspectingly. He changed the subject very abruptly.

"How are the chickens at Farmer Brown's?" inquired he.

Reddy looked up and grinned. "They seem to be in just as good health as ever," said he, "so far as I can judge. Farmer Brown's boy seems to be terribly suspicious. He locks them up at night so tight that not even Shadow the Weasel could get his nose inside that henhouse."

Blacky's eyes twinkled, but he took care that

As Reddy Fox listened, a look of eagerness crept
into his eyes. *See page 78.*

Reddy should not see them. "Farmer Brown's boy is different from some folks I know," said he.

"How's that?" demanded Reddy Fox.

"Why," replied Blacky, "there is a certain farmyard I know of where the hens are not kept shut up at all in the daytime, but run around where they please. I see them every day when I am flying over. They certainly are fine-looking hens. I don't think I've ever seen fatter ones. Some of them are so fat they can hardly run."

As Reddy Fox listened, a look of eagerness crept into his eyes, and his mouth began to water. He just couldn't help it. "Where did you say those hens are?" he asked, trying to speak carelessly.

"I didn't say," replied Blacky, turning his head aside to hide a grin. "It is a long way from here, Reddy, so I don't believe you would really be interested."

"That all depends," replied Reddy. "I would go a long way if it were worth while. I don't suppose you noticed if there were any dogs about where those hens are?"

Blacky pretended not to hear this. "I've often thought," said he, "of you and Mrs. Reddy as I have looked down at those fat hens. It is too bad that they are so far away."

XXVIII
Reddy Fox Dreams of Chickens

It's a poor watch-dog who sleeps with both eyes closed.
Bowser the Hound.

REDDY Fox watched Blacky the Crow grow smaller and smaller until he was just a black speck in the distance. Finally he disappeared. Reddy looked very thoughtful. He looked that way because he *was* thoughtful. In fact, Reddy was doing a lot of hard thinking. He was thinking about those chickens Blacky had told him of. The more he thought of them, the hungrier he grew. You see, Reddy had been having rather a hard time to get enough to eat.

"Yes, Sir," said Reddy to himself, "I would go a long, long distance to get a good plump hen. I wish I knew just where that farm is that that black rascal talked about. I wonder if he has gone that way now. If I were sure that he has, I would make a little journey in that direction myself. But I'm not sure. That black rascal flies all over the country. That farm may lie in the direction he has gone now, and it may be in quite the opposite direction. Somehow I've got to find out in just which direction it is."

Reddy yawned, for he had been out all night, and he was sleepy. He decided that the best thing he could do would be to get a good rest. One must always be fit if one is to get on in this life. The harder one must work, the more fit one should keep, and a proper amount of sleep is one of the most necessary things in keeping fit. So Reddy curled up to sleep.

Hardly had his eyes closed when he began to dream. You see, he had been thinking so hard about those fat hens, and he was so hungry for one of them, that right away he began to dream of fat hens. It was a beautiful dream. At least, it was a beautiful dream to Reddy. Fat hens were all about him. They were so fat that they could hardly walk. Not only were they fat, but they seemed to think that their one object in life was to fill the stomachs of hungry foxes, for they just stood about waiting to be caught.

Never in all his life had Reddy Fox known anything so wonderful as was that dream. There were no dogs to worry him. There were no hunters with dreadful guns. All he had to do was to reach out and help himself to as many fat hens as he wanted. He ate and ate and ate, all in his dream, you know, and when he could eat no more he started for home. When he started for home the fat hens that were left started along with him. He led a procession of fat hens straight over to his home in the Old Pasture.

Just imagine how Reddy felt when at last he awoke and there was not so much as a feather from a fat hen anywhere about, while his stomach fairly ached with emptiness.

XXIX
Reddy Tries to Arouse Blacky's Pity

Trust a Fox only as far as you can see him,
and lock the chickens up before you do that.
Bowser the Hound.

ALL the next night, as Reddy Fox hunted and hunted for something to eat, he kept thinking of that dream of fat hens, and he kept wondering how he could get Blacky the Crow to tell him just where that farm with fat hens was. Blacky on his part had spent a whole day wondering how he could induce Reddy Fox to make that long journey over to where Bowser the Hound was a prisoner of kindness. Blacky was smart enough to know that if he seemed too anxious for Reddy to make that long journey, Reddy would at once suspect something. He knew well enough that if Reddy had any idea that Bowser the Hound was over there, nothing would tempt him to make the trip.

Early the next morning, just as on the morning before, Blacky stopped over by Reddy's house. This time Reddy was already home. Actually he was waiting for Blacky, though he wouldn't have had Blacky know it for the world. As soon as he saw Blacky coming, he lay down on his doorstep and pretended not to see Blacky at all.

"Good morning, Reddy," said Blacky, as he alighted in the top of a little tree close by.

Reddy raised his head as if it were all he could do to lift it. "Good morning, Blacky," said he in a feeble voice.

Blacky looked at him sharply. "What's the matter, Reddy?" he demanded. "You seem to be feeling badly."

Reddy sighed. It was a long, doleful sigh. "I am feeling badly, Blacky," said he. "I never felt worse in my life. The truth is I—I—I—" Reddy paused.

"You what?" demanded Blacky, looking at Reddy more sharply than ever.

"I am starving," said Reddy very feebly. "I certainly shall starve to death unless I can find some way of getting at least one good meal soon. You have no idea, Blacky, how dreadful it is to be hungry all the time." Again Reddy sighed, and followed this with a second sigh and then a third sigh.

Blacky looked behind him so that Reddy might not see the twinkle in his eyes. For Blacky understood perfectly what Reddy was trying to do. Reddy wasn't fooling him a bit. When he looked back at Reddy he was very grave. He was doing his best to look very sympathetic.

"I'm right sorry to hear this, Reddy," said he. "I certainly am. I've been hungry myself more than once. It seems a pity that you should be starving here when over on that farm I told you about yesterday are fat hens to be had for the taking. If you were not so weak, I would be tempted to show you where they are."

XXX
Blacky the Crow Is All Pity

*People who think that they are fooling others very
often discover that they have been fooling themselves.*
Bowser the Hound.

TO have seen and heard Blacky the Crow as he
talked to Reddy Fox, you would have thought
that there was nothing under the sun in his heart
or mind but pity. "Yes, Sir," said he, "I certainly
would be tempted to show you where those fat
hens are if you were not too weak. I just can't bear
to see an old friend starve. It is too bad that those
fat hens are so far away. I feel sure that one of them
would make you quite yourself again."

"Don't—don't talk about them," said Reddy feebly. "If I could have just one fat hen that is all I
would ask. Are they so very far from here?"

Blacky nodded his head vigorously. "Yes," said
he, "they are a long way from here. They are such
a long way that I'm afraid you are too weak to make
the journey. If you were quite yourself you could
do it nicely, but for one in your condition it is, I
fear, altogether too long a journey."

"It wouldn't do any harm to try it, perhaps," sug-
gested Reddy, in a hesitating way. "It is no worse to
starve to death in one place than another, and I
never was one to give up without trying. If you

85

don't mind showing me the way, Brother Blacky, I would at least like to try to reach that place where the fat hens are. Of course I cannot keep up with you. In fact, I couldn't if I were feeling well and strong. Perhaps you can tell me just how to find that place, and then I needn't bother you at all."

Blacky pretended to be lost in thought while Reddy watched him anxiously. Finally Blacky spoke. "It certainly makes my heart ache to see you in such a condition, Brother Reddy," said he. "I tell you what I'll do. You know we Crows are famous for flying in a straight line when we want to get to any place in particular. I will fly straight towards that farm where the fat hens are. You follow along as best you can. In your feeble condition it will take you a long time to get anywhere near there. This will give me time to go hunt for my own dinner, and then I will come back until I meet you. After that, I will show you the way. Now I will start along and you follow."

Reddy got to his feet as if it were hard work. Then Blacky spread his wings and started off, cawing encouragement. All the time inside he was laughing to think that Reddy Fox should think he had fooled him. "He forgot to ask again if there is a dog there," chuckled Blacky to himself.

As for Reddy, no sooner was Blacky well on his way than he started off at his swiftest pace. There was nothing weak or feeble in the way Reddy ran then. He was in a hurry to get to those fat hens.

XXXI
Blacky Is Much Pleased with Himself

*You cannot tell from a single feather what a bird looks like,
nor from a lone hair how big a dog is.*
                                                    Bowser the Hound.

STRAIGHT away towards the farm where Bowser
the Hound was flew Blacky the Crow. Every few
minutes he would caw encouragement to Reddy
Fox, who, as you know, was following, but who of
course could not travel as fast as did Blacky. In
between times Blacky would chuckle to himself.
He was mightily pleased with himself, was Blacky.

In the first place his plan was working beautiful-
ly. You know what he was after was to get Reddy
Fox over to that farm where Bowser was. He hoped
that if Reddy should catch one of those fat hens,
the farmer would put Bowser on Reddy's trail. He
knew that Reddy would probably return straight
home, and Bowser, following Reddy's trail, would
thus find his way back home to Farmer Brown's. Of
course, it all depended on whether Reddy would
catch one of those fat hens and whether Bowser
would be allowed to hunt him. Blacky had a plan
for making sure that if Reddy did get one of those
hens the folks in the farmhouse would know it.

But what tickled Blacky most was the knowledge that Reddy Fox thought he was fooling Blacky. You remember that Reddy had pretended to be very weak. Blacky knew that Reddy was nothing of the kind. At the very first opportunity Blacky stopped in the top of a tall tree as if to rest. His real reason for stopping was to have a chance to look back. You see, while he was flying he couldn't look behind him.

Presently, just as he expected, he saw in the distance a little red speck, and that little red speck was moving very fast indeed. There was nothing weak or feeble in the way that red speck was coming across the snow-covered fields. Blacky chuckled hoarsely.

Nearer and nearer came the red speck, and of course the nearer it came the larger it grew. Presently it stopped moving fast. It began to move slowly and stop every once in a while, as if to rest. Blacky laughed right out. He knew then that Reddy Fox had discovered him sitting in the top of that tall tree and was once more pretending. It was a sort of a game, a game that Blacky thoroughly enjoyed.

As soon as he knew that Reddy had discovered him, he once more spread his black wings and started on. The same thing happened over again. In fact, Blacky did not fly far this time before once more waiting. It was great fun to see Reddy suddenly pretend that he was too weak to run. It was such fun that Blacky quite forgot that he had had no breakfast.

Yes, Blacky the Crow was very much pleased with himself. It looked very much as if he would succeed in helping Bowser the Hound. This pleased him. But it pleased him still more to know that he was fooling clever Reddy Fox while Reddy thought he was the one who was doing the fooling.

XXXII
Blacky Waits for Reddy

Be wise, my friends, and do not fail
To trust a dog who wags his tail.
          Bowser the Hound.

JUST before reaching the farm where the fat hens
and Bowser the Hound were, Blacky waited for
Reddy Fox to catch up. It was some time before
Reddy appeared, for he wasn't traveling as fast
now as when he had started out. You see, that farm
really was a very long way from the Old Pasture
where Reddy lives and Reddy had run very hard,
because, you know, he was so anxious to get one of
those fat hens.

As soon as Blacky saw him he hid in the thick
branches of a tall pine-tree. Reddy didn't see him.
In fact, Blacky had been so far ahead that Reddy
had lost sight of him some time before. Out of the
bushes trotted Reddy. His tongue was hanging out
just a little, and he was panting. Blacky was just
about to speak when Reddy stopped. He stood as
still as if he had suddenly been frozen stiff. His
sharp black ears were cocked forward, and his
head was turned just a little to one side. Reddy was
listening. He was listening for the voice of Blacky.

90

You see, he thought Blacky was still far ahead of him.

For several minutes Reddy stood listening with all his might, and Blacky's sharp eyes twinkled as he looked down, watching Reddy. Suddenly Reddy sat down. There was an expression on his sharp face which Blacky understood perfectly. It was quite plain that Reddy was becoming suspicious. He had begun to suspect that he had been tricked by Blacky and led so far away from home for nothing.

Down inside Blacky chuckled. It was a noiseless chuckle, for Blacky did not intend to give himself away until he had to. But when at last he saw that Reddy was beginning to get uneasy, Blacky spoke. "You seem to be feeling better, Brother Reddy," said he. "You must excuse me for keeping you waiting, but I did not suppose that any one so weak and feeble as you appeared to be early this morning could possibly get here so soon."

At the sound of Blacky's voice, Reddy was so startled that he jumped quite as if he had sat down on a prickly briar. He was sharp enough to know that it was no longer of any use to pretend. "I'm feeling better," said he. "The thought of those fat hens has quite restored my strength. Did you say that they are near here?"

"I didn't say, but—" Blacky didn't finish. He didn't need to. From the other side of a little swamp in front of them a rooster crowed. That was answer enough. Reddy's yellow eyes gleamed. In an instant he was on his feet, the picture of alertness.

"Are you satisfied that I told the truth?" asked Blacky. Reddy nodded.

XXXIII
Reddy Watches the Fat Hens

Sooner or later the crookedest trail will straighten.
Bowser the Hound.

A T the sound of that rooster's voice on the other side of the little swamp, Reddy became a changed Fox. Could you have been sitting where you could have seen him, as did Blacky the Crow, you never, never would have guessed that Reddy had run a very long distance and was tired. He did not even glance up at Blacky. He did not even say thank you to Blacky for having shown him the way. He looked neither to the right nor to the left, but with eyes fixed eagerly ahead, began to steal forward swiftly.

Making no sound, for Reddy can step very lightly when he chooses to, he trotted quickly through the little swamp until he drew near the other side. Then he crouched close to the snow-covered ground and began to steal from bush to bush until he reached the trunk of a fallen tree on the very edge of the swamp. To this he crawled on his stomach and peeped around the end of it.

Everything was as Blacky the Crow had said. Not far away was a farmyard, and walking about in it was a big rooster, lording it over a large flock of fat hens. They were not shut in by a wire fence as were Farmer Brown's hens. Some were taking a sun bath just in front of the barn door. Others were scattered about, picking up bits of food which had been thrown out for them. A few were scratching in some straw in the cowyard. In the barn a horse stamped. From the farmhouse sounded the voice of a woman singing. Once the door of the farmhouse opened, and an appetizing odor floated out to tickle the nose of Reddy.

Reddy looked sharply for signs of a dog. Not one could he see. If there was a dog, he must be either in the barn or in the house. It was quite clear to Reddy that no Fox had bothered this flock of fat hens. He was sorely tempted to rush out and grab one of them at once, but he didn't. He was far too clever to do anything like that until he was absolutely sure that it would be safe.

So Reddy lay flat behind the old tree trunk, with just his nose and his eyes showing around the end of it, and studied what would be best to do. He was sure that he could get one of those fat hens, but he wanted more. Early that morning Reddy would have been quite contented with one, but now that he was sure that he could get one, he wanted more. If he were too bold and frightened those hens while catching one, they would make such a racket that they would be sure to bring some one from the farmhouse. The thing to do was to be patient until he could catch one without alarming the others. Then perhaps he would be able to catch another. Reddy decided to be patient and wait.

XXXIV
Patience and Impatience

Patience is a virtue
In a cause that's right.
In a cause that isn't,
It's a cause for fright.
Bowser the Hound.

ONE of the first things that the little people of
the Green Forest and the Green Meadows who
hunt other little people learn is patience. Sometimes it takes a long time to learn this, but it is a
necessary lesson. Reddy Fox had learned it. Reddy
knew that often even his cleverness would not succeed without patience. When he was young he had
lost many a good meal through impatience.

Reddy could not remember when he had been
more hungry than he was now. Lying there behind
the fallen tree, watching the fat hens walking about
unsuspectingly just a little way from him, it
seemed to him that he simply must rush out and
catch one of them. But Reddy was smart enough to
know that if he did this there would at once be
such a screaming and squawking that some one
would be sure to rush out from the farmhouse to
find out what was going on. If he were discovered,
there would be small chance for him to get another
fat hen. Reddy is keen enough to make the most of

96

an opportunity. He knew that if he could get one of these hens without frightening the others, he would have a chance to get another. He might have a chance to get several in this way.

So, though he was so eager and so hungry, he made himself keep perfectly still, while he studied out a plan. By and by he stole ever so carefully around back of the barn to the cowyard. Some of those fat hens were scratching in the straw of the cowyard. Just outside the cowyard was a pile of old boards. Reddy crawled behind this pile of old boards and then crouched and settled himself to be patient. He knew that sooner or later one of those fat hens would be likely to come out of the cowyard. In this way he might be able to catch one without the others knowing a thing about it.

Blacky the Crow sat in the top of a tall tree where he could see all that was going on. Blacky was as impatient as Reddy was patient. "Why doesn't the red rascal rush in and get one of those fat hens?" muttered Blacky. "What is the matter with him, anyway? I wonder if he is afraid. He could catch one of them without half trying, and there he lies as if he expected them to run right into his mouth. I don't want to sit here all day. Yet I can't do a thing until he catches one of those hens."

So Reddy waited patiently and Blacky waited impatiently, and the fat hens wandered about unsuspectingly, and for a long, long time nothing happened.

XXXV
Things Happen All At Once

*The cleverest Fox is almost certain to visit
the chicken yard once too often.*
Bowser the Hound.

JOLLY, round, bright Mr. Sun, high in the blue,
blue sky, looked down on as peaceful a scene as
ever was. In the cowyard back of the barn of this
particular farm stood several cows contentedly
chewing their cuds as they took their daily airing.
Half a dozen fat hens were walking about among
them and scratching in the straw. Out in the farmyard in front of the barn were many more fat hens.
Behind a pile of old boards just outside the cowyard was a spot of red. In the top of a tall tree not
far distant was a spot of black. The smoke from the
chimney of the farmhouse floated skyward in a
lazy way. Looking down on the Great World, jolly,
round, bright Mr. Sun saw no more peaceful scene
anywhere.

By and by a fat hen walked over to the bars of
the cowyard and hopped up on the lower bar.
There she sat for some time. Then, making up her
mind that she would see what was outside, she
hopped down and walked over to the pile of old

boards. Right then things happened all at once. That red spot behind the pile of old boards suddenly came to life. There was a quick spring, and that fat hen was seized by the neck so suddenly that she didn't have time to make a sound. At the same instant the black spot in the top of the tall tree came to life, and Blacky the Crow flew over to the roof of the barn, screaming at the top of his lungs. Now those who know Blacky well, know when he is screaming "Fox! Fox! Fox!" although it sounds as if he were saying "Caw! Caw! Caw!"

In a moment the door of the farmhouse flew open, and a man stepped out with a dog at his heels. The man looked up at Blacky, and he knew by Blacky's actions that something was going on back of the barn. Right away he guessed that there must be a Fox there, and calling the dog to follow, he ran around to see what was happening. Of course Reddy heard him coming, and with a little snarl of anger at Blacky the Crow, he seized the fat hen by the neck, threw her body over his shoulder, and started for the near-by swamp as fast as his legs could take him.

Just as Reddy reached the edge of the swamp, he heard the roar of a great voice behind him. He knew that voice. It was the voice of Bowser the Hound. It could be no one else but Bowser who was behind him, for there was no other voice quite like his. Dismay awoke in Reddy's heart. He knew that Bowser was wise to the tricks of Foxes, and that he would have to use all his cunning to get rid of Bowser. To do it he would have to drop that fat hen he had come so far to get. Do you wonder that Reddy was dismayed?

XXXVI
Reddy Hides the Fat Hen

Dishonesty will run away
Where Honesty will boldly stay.
Bowser the Hound.

REDDY Fox was in a fix! He certainly was in a fix! Here he was with the fat hen which he had come such a long, long way to get, and no chance to eat it, for Bowser the Hound was on his trail. Ordinarily Reddy Fox can run faster than can Bowser, but it is one thing to run with nothing to carry, and another thing altogether to run with a burden as heavy as a fat hen. Reddy's wits were working quite as fast as his legs.

"I can't carry this fat hen far," thought Reddy, "for Bowser will surely catch me. I don't want to drop it, because I have come such a long way to get it, and goodness knows when I will be able to catch another. The thing for me to do is to hide it where I can come back and get it after I get rid of that pesky dog. Goodness, what a noise he makes!"

As he ran, Reddy watched sharply this way and that way for a place to hide the fat hen. He knew he must find a place soon, because already that fat hen was growing very heavy. Presently he spied

the hollow stump of a tree. He didn't know it was
hollow when he first saw it, but from its looks he
thought it might be. The top of it was only about
two feet above the ground. Reddy stopped and
stood up on his hind legs so as to see if the top of
that stump was hollow. It was. With a quick look
this way and that way to make sure he wasn't seen,
he tossed the fat hen over into the hollow and
then, with a sigh of relief, darted away.

With the weight of that fat hen off his shoulders,
and the worry about it off his mind, Reddy could
give all his attention to getting rid of Bowser the
Hound. He had no intention of running any farther
than he must. In the first place he had traveled so
far that he did not feel like running. In the second
place he wanted to get back to that hollow stump
and the fat hen just as soon as possible.

It wasn't long before Reddy realized that it was
not going to be so easy to fool Bowser the Hound.
Bowser was too wise to be fooled by common
tricks such as breaking the trail by jumping far to
one side after running back on his own tracks a little way; or by running along a fallen tree and jumping from the end of it as far as he could. Of course
he tried these tricks, but each time Bowser simply
made a big circle with his nose to the ground and
picked up Reddy's new trail.

Reddy didn't know that country about there at
all, and little by little he began to realize how much
this meant. At home he knew every foot of the

ground for a long distance in every direction. This made all the difference in the world, because he knew just how to play all kinds of tricks. But here it was different. It seemed to him that all he could do was to run and run.

XXXVII
Farmer Brown's Boy Has a Glad Surprise

The sweetest sound in the world is the voice
of one you love.
Bowser the Hound.

FARMER Brown's boy had an errand which took
him far from home. He harnessed the horse to a
sleigh and started off right after dinner. Now it happened that his errand took him in the direction of
the farm where Bowser the Hound had been taken
such good care of, and where Reddy Fox had that
very day caught the fat hen. Farmer Brown's boy
was not thinking of Bowser. You see, he had
already visited most of the farms in that direction
in his search for Bowser and had found no trace of
him.

It was a beautiful day to be sleighing, and Farmer
Brown's boy was whistling merrily, for there is
nothing he enjoys more than a sleigh ride. He had
almost reached the place he had started for when
'way off across the fields to his right he heard a
dog. Now Farmer Brown's boy enjoys listening to
the sound of a Hound chasing a Fox. There is something about it which stirs the blood. He stopped
whistling and stopped the horse in order that he
might listen better.

At first that sound was very, very faint, but as Farmer Brown's boy listened, it grew louder and clearer. Suddenly Farmer Brown's boy leaped up excitedly. "That's Bowser!" he cried. "As sure as I live that's good old Bowser! I would know that voice among a million!"

He leaped from the sleigh and tied the horse. Then he climbed over the fence and began to run across the snow-covered fields. He could tell from the sound in what direction Bowser was running. He could tell from the appearance of the country about where Reddy Fox would be likely to lead Bowser, and he ran for a place which he felt sure Reddy would be likely to pass.

Louder and louder sounded the great voice of Bowser, and faster and faster ran Farmer Brown's boy to reach that place before Bowser should pass. Thc louder that great voice sounded, the more absolutely certain Farmer Brown's boy became that it was the voice of Bowser, and a great joy filled his heart. At last he reached an old road. He felt certain that Reddy would follow that road. So he hid behind an old stone wall on the edge of it.

He did not have long to wait. A red form appeared around a turn in the old road, running swiftly. Then it stopped and stood perfectly still. Of course it was Reddy Fox. He was listening to make sure just how far behind him Bowser was. He listened for only a moment and then started on as swiftly as before. Right down the road past Farmer Brown's boy Reddy ran, and never once suspected he was being watched.

A few minutes later another form appeared around the turn in the road. It was Bowser! Yes, Sir, it was Bowser! With a glad cry Farmer Brown's boy jumped over the stone wall and waited.

XXXVIII
Reddy Goes Back for His Fat Hen

Joy will make a puppy of an old dog.
Bowser the Hound.

WHEN Bowser the Hound is following the trail
of Reddy Fox, it takes a great deal to make
him leave that trail. His love of the hunt is so great
that, as a rule, nothing short of losing the trail will
make him stop. He will follow it until he cannot follow it any longer.

But for once Bowser actually forgot that he was
following Reddy Fox. Yes, Sir, he did. As he came
down that old road with his nose in Reddy's tracks,
he was so intent on what he was doing that he
didn't see Farmer Brown's boy waiting for him. He
didn't see him until he almost ran into him.

For just a second Bowser stared in utter surprise. Then with a little yelp of pure joy he leaped
up and did his best to lick his master's face. Could
you have seen Bowser, you might have thought
that he was just a foolish young puppy, he cut up
such wild antics to express his joy. He yelped and
whined and barked. He nearly knocked Farmer
Brown's boy down by leaping up on him. He raced
around in circles. When at last he was still long

enough, Farmer Brown's boy just threw his arms around him and hugged him. He hugged him so hard he made Bowser squeal. Then two of the happiest folks in all the Great World started back across the snow-covered fields to the sleigh.

Bowser and Farmer Brown's boy were not the only ones who rejoiced. Reddy Fox had been badly worried. Although he had tried every trick he could think of, he had not been able to get rid of Bowser, and he had just about made up his mind that there was nothing for it but to start back to the Old Pasture which was so far away. That would mean giving up the fat hen which he had hidden in the hollow stump.

Of course, Reddy knew the instant that Bowser began to yelp and bark that something had happened. What it was he couldn't imagine. He sat down to wait and listen. Then he heard the voice of Farmer Brown's boy. Reddy knew that voice and he grinned, for he felt sure that Bowser would give up the hunt. He grinned because now he would have a chance to go back for that fat hen. At the same time that grin was not wholly a happy grin, because Reddy knew that now Bowser would return to his home.

Presently Reddy very carefully crept back to a place where he could see what was going on. He watched Farmer Brown's boy start back for the road and the sleigh, with Bowser jumping up on him and racing around him like a foolish young puppy. He waited only long enough to make sure that Bowser would not come back; then he turned and trotted swiftly along his own back trail towards that hollow stump into which he had tossed that fat hen. Reddy's thoughts were very pleasant thoughts, for they were all of the fine dinner of which he now felt sure.

XXXIX
A Vanished Dinner

This fact you'll find where'er you go
Is true of Fox or Dog or Man:
Dishonesty has never paid,
And, what is more, it never can.
Bowser the Hound.

VERY pleasant were the thoughts of Reddy Fox as he trotted back to the swamp where was the hollow stump in which he had hidden the fat hen he had stolen. Yes, Sir, very pleasant were the thoughts of Reddy Fox. He felt sure that no dinner he had ever eaten had tasted anywhere near as good as would the dinner he was about to enjoy.

In the first place his stomach had not been really filled for a long time. Food had been scarce, and while Reddy had always obtained enough to keep from starving, it was a long time since he had had a really good meal. He had, you remember, traveled a very long distance to catch that fat hen, and it had been many hours since he had had a bite of anything. There is nothing like a good appetite to make things taste good. Reddy certainly had the appetite to make that fat hen the finest dinner a Fox ever ate.

So, with pleasant thoughts of the feast to come,

Reddy trotted along swiftly. Presently he reached the little swamp in which was the hollow stump. As he drew near it, he moved very carefully. You see, he was not quite sure that all was safe. He knew that the farmer from whom he had stolen that fat hen had seen him run away with it, and he feared that that farmer might be hiding somewhere about with a terrible gun. So Reddy used his eyes and his ears and his nose as only he can use them. All seemed safe. It was as still in that little swamp as if no living creature had ever visited it. Stopping every few steps to look, listen, and sniff, Reddy approached that hollow stump.

Quite certain in his own mind that there was no danger, Reddy lightly leaped up on the old stump and peeped into the hollow in the top. Then he blinked his eyes very fast indeed. If ever there has been a surprised Fox in all the Great World that one was Reddy. There was no fat hen in that hollow! Reddy couldn't believe it. He *wouldn't* believe it. That fat hen just *had* to be there. He blinked his eyes some more and looked again. All he saw in that hollow stump was a feather. The fat hen had vanished. All Reddy's dreams of a good dinner vanished too. A great rage took their place. Somebody had *stolen* his fat hen!

Reddy looked about him hurriedly and anxiously. There wasn't a sign of anybody about, or that anybody had been there. Reddy's anger began to give place to wonder and then to something very like fear. How could anybody have taken that fat hen and left no trace? And how could a fat hen with a broken neck disappear of its own accord? It gave Reddy a creepy feeling.

XL
Where Was Reddy's Dinner?

*Often it is better to look for a new trail than
to waste time hunting for an old one.*
Bowser the Hound.

REDDY Fox is used to all sorts of queer happenings. Yes, Sir, he is used to all sorts of queer happenings, and as a rule Reddy is seldom puzzled for long. You see he is such a clever fellow himself that any one clever enough to fool him for long must be very clever indeed. This time, however, all the cleverness of his sharp wits did him no good. The fat hen he had hidden in a hollow stump had disappeared without leaving a trace.

Reddy's first thought was that probably the farmer from whom he had stolen the fat hen had found it and taken it away. At once he began to use that wonderful nose of his searching for the scent of that farmer. Very carefully he sniffed all about the top of that old stump and inside the hollow. There wasn't the faintest scent of anybody there. Then he jumped down, and with his nose to the ground, ran all around the stump, sniffing, sniffing, sniffing. The only thing he discovered was the scent of Bowser the Hound, and he knew that Bowser had not taken that fat hen, because, as you remember, Bowser had kept right on chasing him.

Reddy began to feel afraid of that old stump. People usually are afraid of mysterious things, and it certainly was very mysterious that a fat hen with a broken neck should disappear without leaving any trace at all. Reddy sat down at a little distance and did a lot of hard thinking. He looked every which way, even up in the tree tops, but all his looking was in vain. It was so mysterious that if he hadn't known positively that he was awake he would have thought it was all a dream.

But Reddy is something of a philosopher. That fat hen was gone, and there was no use in wasting time puzzling over it. There were other fat hens where that one came from, and he would just have to catch another.

So Reddy trotted through the swamp till he came to the edge of it. There his keen nose found the scent of the farmer. It didn't take him two minutes to discover that the farmer had followed Bowser the Hound to the edge of the swamp and then gone back. Eagerly Reddy looked over to the farmyard for those fat hens. They, too, had disappeared. Not one was to be seen. But there was no mystery about the disappearance of these other fat hens. He heard the muffled crow of the big rooster. It came from the henhouse. All those fat hens had been shut up. It was perfectly plain to Reddy that the farmer suspected Reddy might return, and he didn't intend to lose another fat hen. With a little yelp of disappointment, Reddy turned his back on the farm and trotted off into the woods.

XLI
What Blacky the Crow Saw

The greatest puzzle is simple enough
when you know the answer.
Bowser the Hound.

THERE were just two people to whom the disappearance of that fat hen Reddy Fox had hidden in the hollow stump was not a mystery. One of them was Blacky the Crow. When the farmer and Bowser the Hound had rushed out at the sound of Blacky's excited cawing, Blacky had flown to the top of a tall tree from which he could see all that went on. Everything had happened just as Blacky had hoped it would. Bowser had taken the trail of Reddy Fox, and Blacky felt sure that sooner or later Reddy would lead him back home to Farmer Brown's.

Blacky was doubly pleased with himself. He was pleased to think that he had found a way of getting Bowser back home, and he was quite as much pleased because he had been smart enough to outwit Reddy Fox. He didn't wish Reddy any harm, and he felt sure that no harm would come to him. He didn't even wish him to lose that dinner Reddy had come so far to get, but he didn't care if Reddy did lose it, if only his plan worked out as he hoped it would.

"I wonder what he'll do with that fat hen," mut-

tered Blacky, as he watched Reddy race away with
it thrown over his shoulders. "He can't carry that
hen far and keep out of the way of Bowser. I think
I'll follow and see what he does with it."

So Blacky followed, and his eyes twinkled when
he saw Reddy hide the fat hen in the hollow stump.
He knew that no matter how far Bowser might
chase Reddy, Reddy would come back for that fat
hen, and he was rather glad to think that Reddy
would have that good dinner after all.

"No one will ever think to look in that hollow
stump," thought Blacky, "and I certainly will not
tell any one. Reddy has earned that dinner. Now I
think I'll go get something to eat myself."

At that very instant Blacky's sharp eyes caught a
glimpse of a gray form with broad wings, and in a
perfect panic of fear Blacky began to fly as fast as
he knew how for a thick spruce-tree not far away.
He plunged in among the branches and hid in the
thickest part he could find. With little shivers of
fear running all over him, he peeked out and
watched that big gray form. On broad wings it
sailed over to that hollow stump. Two long legs
with great curving claws reached down in, and a
moment later that fat hen was disappearing over
the tree tops. Blacky sighed with relief.

"It's a lucky thing for me that robber, Mr.
Goshawk, saw Reddy hide that fat hen," muttered
Blacky. "If he hadn't, he might have caught me, for
I didn't see him at all."

On broad wings it sailed over to that hollow stump.
See page 116.

XLII
All Is Well That Ends Well

When things go wrong, just patient be
Until the end you plainly see.
For often things that seem all bad
Will end by making all hands glad.
Bowser the Hound.

REDDY Fox, trotting homeward, had nothing but bitterness in his heart, and nothing at all in his stomach. He was tired and hungry and bitterly disappointed. He was in a country with which he was not familiar, and so he did not know where to hunt, and he felt that he just must get something to eat. Do what he would, he couldn't help thinking about that fat hen he had hidden and which had so mysteriously disappeared. The more he thought of it, the worse he felt. It was bad enough to be hungry and have no idea where the next meal was coming from, but it was many times worse to have had that meal and then lose it. To Reddy, everything was all wrong.

Now on his way home Reddy had to pass several farms. Hunger made him bold, and at each farm he stole softly as near as possible to the farmyard, hoping that he might find more fat hens unguarded. Now it happened that that afternoon a farmer at one of these farms was preparing some chickens to be taken to market early the next morning. He was picking these chickens in a shed attached to the barn. He had several all picked when he was called to the house on an errand.

It happened that just after he had disappeared Reddy Fox came stealing around from behind the barn, and at once he smelled those chickens. Just imagine how Reddy felt when he peeped in that shed and saw those fine chickens just waiting for him. Two minutes later Reddy was racing back to the woods with one of them. This time there was no dog behind him. And in a little hollow Reddy ate the finest dinner he ever had had. You see there were no feathers to bother him on that chicken, for it had been picked. When the last bit had disappeared, Reddy once more started for home, and this time he was happy, for his stomach was full.

Long before Reddy got back to the Old Pasture Farmer Brown's boy and Bowser the Hound had reached home. Such a fuss as everybody did make over Bowser. It seemed as if each one at Farmer Brown's was trying to spoil Bowser. As for Bowser himself, he was the happiest dog in all the Great World.

Blacky the Crow got back to the Green Forest near Farmer Brown's just before jolly, round Mr. Sun went to bed. Blacky had found plenty to eat and he had seen no more of fierce Mr. Goshawk. As Blacky settled himself on his roost he heard from the direction of Farmer Brown's house a great voice. It was the voice of Bowser the Hound trying to express his joy in being home. Blacky chuckled contentedly. He, too, was happy, for it always makes one happy to have one's plans succeed.

"All's well that end's well," he chuckled, and closed his eyes sleepily.

Blacky never could have fooled old Granny Fox as he did Reddy. She is far too smart to be fooled even by so clever a scamp as Blacky. She is so smart that she deserves a book all her own, and so the next volume in this series will be Old Granny Fox.

THE END